Balloons
Balloons
Balloons

by **Dee Lillegard**

illustrated by
Bernadette Pons

Dutton Children's Books

DUTTON CHILDREN'S BOOKS
A division of Penguin Young Readers Group

Published by the Penguin Group

Penguin Group (USA) Inc., 375 Hudson Street, New York, New York 10014, U.S.A.
Penguin Group (Canada), 90 Eglinton Avenue East, Suite 700, Toronto, Ontario, Canada M4P 2Y3
(a division of Pearson Penguin Canada Inc.)
Penguin Books Ltd, 80 Strand, London WC2R 0RL, England
Penguin Ireland, 25 St Stephen's Green, Dublin 2, Ireland (a division of Penguin Books Ltd)
Penguin Group (Australia), 250 Camberwell Road, Camberwell, Victoria 3124, Australia
(a division of Pearson Australia Group Pty Ltd)
Penguin Books India Pvt Ltd, 11 Community Centre, Panchsheel Park, New Delhi - 110 017, India
Penguin Group (NZ), Cnr Airborne and Rosedale Roads, Albany, Auckland 1310, New Zealand
(a division of Pearson New Zealand Ltd)
Penguin Books (South Africa) (Pty) Ltd, 24 Sturdee Avenue, Rosebank, Johannesburg 2196, South Africa
Penguin Books Ltd, Registered Offices: 80 Strand, London WC2R 0RL, England

CIP Data is available.

Published in the United States by Dutton Children's Books,
a division of Penguin Young Readers Group
345 Hudson Street, New York, New York 10014
www.penguin.com/youngreaders

Designed by Beth Herzog

Manufactured in China
First Edition
ISBN 978-0-525-45940-8
10 9 8 7 6 5 4 3 2 1

To Aden, Gabriella, and Selena
— D.L.

To Janet, Mark, Sophie, and Jonas
— B.P.

Snap snap
Clap clap
Balloons Balloons Balloons

A raspberry red one
A blueberry blue one
Shiny as a shoe one
Balloons Balloons Balloons

A yum yummy yellow one
A plum plummy purple one
A green like a turtle one
Balloons Balloons Balloons

Selena gets a pink one
A squiddy-black-ink one
A white as a sink one
Balloons Balloons Balloons

Izzy wants a silver
Gabby wants a gold
Balloons Balloons Balloons
Too many to hold

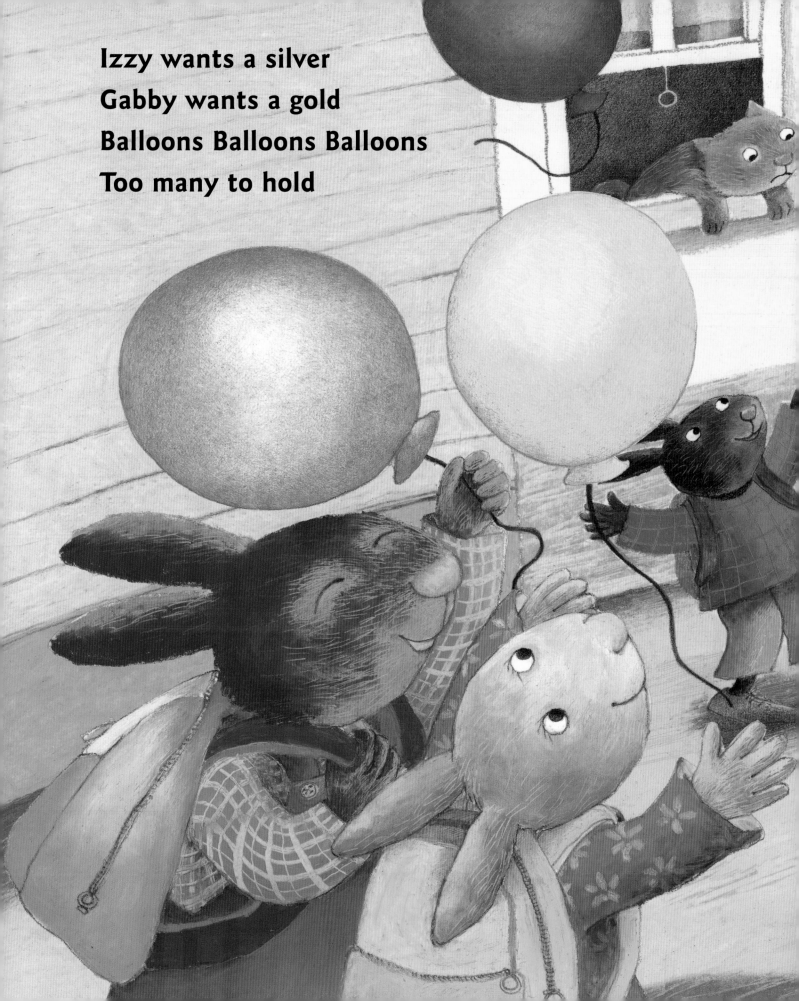

Aaron has an orange
Aden has a brown
Balloons Balloons Balloons
Coloring the town

Snap snap
Clap clap
Balloons Balloons Balloons

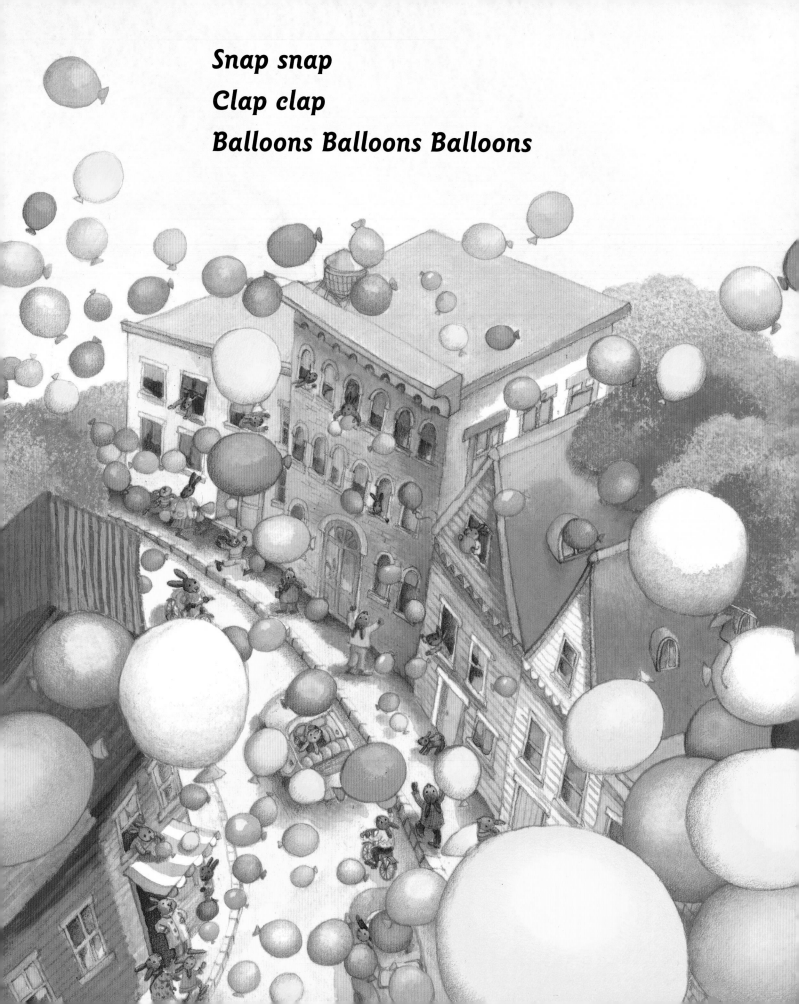

Balloons on the sidewalks
Balloons in the streets
Balloons on the corner
Where everyone meets

Balloons at the window
Balloons at the door
Balloons in the aisles
At the grocery store

Balloons on cereals
Jellies and jams
Balloons on veggies
On cheeses and hams

Balloons in buildings
Balloons on chairs
Balloons in elevators
Balloons on stairs

Balloons on the tennis court
Balloons at the pool
Balloons on the bus

Balloons go to school!

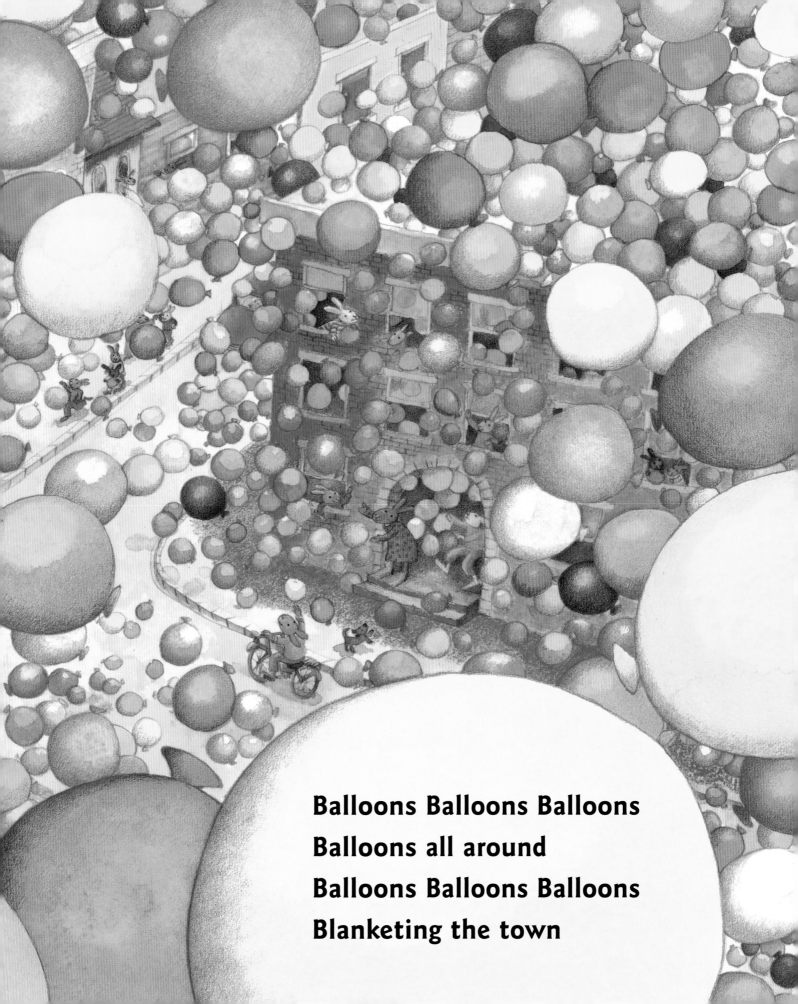

Balloons Balloons Balloons
Balloons all around
Balloons Balloons Balloons
Blanketing the town

Snap snap
Clap clap
Balloons Balloons Balloons

Balloons like a rocket
Rising in the sky
Zoom zoom zoom
Soaring higher than high

Fly away

Fly away

To other suns and moons

Balloons Balloons
Balloons Balloons
Balloons Balloons Balloons